MONTY'S JOURNEY

MONTY'S JOURNEY

Paul Geraghty

Collins

An Imprint of HarperCollins*Publishers*

for Stef, Sue, Mark and Kim

First published by HarperCollins 1992
© text & illustrations Paul Geraghty 1992

9 8 7 6 5 4 3 2

A CIP catalogue record for this book
is available from the British Library
The Author asserts the moral right to
be identified as the author of this work.

Printed and bound in Great Britain
by BPCC Paulton Books

This book is set in Times 18/23

A little girl riding in the country
had a parcel in her basket. In the
parcel were Monty and
his friends.

They were moving
to a place called
Town. They had
heard it was
jam packed with
bangers and big
cheeses with lots
of dough. It
sounded like just
the place for them.

Their journey was going smoothly,
but then they hit a bump.

Out fell Monty! He
tumbled and crashed
and bounced and
bumped while the
bicycle and the parcel
sped away.
"Wait for me!" he cried.
"Wait!" But they didn't;
they left him behind.

Lost and alone he sat, reflecting miserably, when a beetle floated by. It gave him a brilliant idea.

"Of course," he thought,
"this old carton will float
to Town – with me inside."
And he jumped in.

He was sailing along happily until two people thought his boat was a piece of old rubbish.

Now he was really down in the dumps and worse still, the bag was jolting and bumping about. Monty wanted to escape.

Then the jolting
and bumping stopped
but a tugging feeling
began. It was another
creature – a big one.

With a rip, Monty burst free,
but he didn't like what
he saw.

And it was so noisy
and wet. Monty
saw his moment
to escape
and took it ...

...only Monty couldn't
swim.

He flung his arms in all directions until at last he
found something to cling to. From somewhere
outside he could hear a voice.

"The train on platform two is
calling at all stations to Town."
"What luck!" Monty thought,
scrambling out towards the
light. And dodging the rush,
he took a mighty leap.

But boarding a train wasn't quite as easy ...

... as it looked.

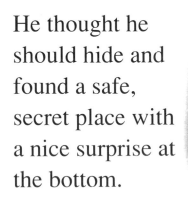

He thought he
should hide and
found a safe,
secret place with
a nice surprise at
the bottom.

Then the train stopped, and he was taken for a walk. "This must be Town," he thought.

When he had seen enough of Town, he
was hung up in a house.

Getting down from his safe place
was easy, but getting away wasn't!

Fortunately, he spotted an escape route.

Unfortunately, it
was occupied.

Monty closed his eyes and took an
enormous leap...
...and landed in a trifle.
"MONTY!" his friends all squeaked,
"You're here!"
"Sorry to drop in like this," he said,
"but I had to get away from the rat race."

"How did you find us?" they asked.
"Oh, it was a piece of cake," he said, and
they all laughed. Then they sang 'For He's a
Jolly Good Mouse', and threw a noisy party that
kept their enemies awake all night. "I think I'm
going to like Town,"
thought Monty.